Klee Wyck's Magic Quest

Sonia Birch-Jones

Illustrated by **Lissa Calvert**

Klee Wyck™
O F F I C I A L   M A S C O T
XV Commonwealth Games
XV Jeux du Commonwealth

OOLICHAN BOOKS
Lantzville, British Columbia, Canada

Publication assistance provided by the Canada Council.

Acknowledgements
The author wishes to thank Karel Loganhume, Anna Maria Wood, Dr. Gwyneth Evans, Dr. Terry Johnson, Rhonda Bailey and Ron and Pat Smith for their encouragement and assistance.
   Special thanks to my daughters Beverly and Brooke, to Lissa for sharing her considerable talent, and to Peter, my husband, for his understanding.

Canadian Cataloguing in Publication Data

Birch-Jones, Sonia, 1921-
   Klee Wyck's magic quest

   ISBN 0-88982-127-5

   I. Calvert, Lissa.   II. Title.
PS8553.I72K5 1993   JC813'.54   C93-091288-8
PZ7.B57K1 1993

Design by Jim Bennett of Morriss Printing Company Ltd., Victoria, British Columbia, Canada
Printed and bound in Canada by Friesen Printers

Published by **oolichan books**
Box 10, Lantzville, British Columbia, Canada   VOR 2HO

To my grandchildren
Because all children are magic

*O*ne sunny morning, Klee Wyck, a young Orca, was beach rubbing at Robson Bight. Along with the other great black and white whales in her pod, Klee Wyck rubbed her sides and belly on the smooth pebbles. As she moved back and forth, her Commonwealth Games Gold Medal sparkled at the end of a beautiful red and blue ribbon that hung around her neck. The medal had been given to Klee Wyck when she was made the 1994 Commonwealth Games mascot, and she was very proud of it. In a short while she would wear it to the opening of the Games.

Charlotte, Klee Wyck's mother and the leader of the pod, shifted beside her daughter. "Time to go," she said. "We must feed before the sun sets." Propelling themselves with their flukes, the big mammals slid back through the shallows to deeper water. There they began to dive for food.

But while Klee Wyck and her young brother Kia were diving a dreadful thing happened. The ribbon snapped. Away drifted the gold medal. Klee Wyck swam desperately after it and little Kia followed. "Go back," called Klee Wyck. But the mischievous one-year-old ignored her.

The water became cloudy. Klee Wyck could barely see the medal, which fell rapidly. Suddenly a clawlike hand reached out and grabbed it. Klee Wyck hesitated, but Kia swam past her, right into the cave of Hagema, the evil sea witch.

Klee Wyck tried to follow Kia, but two giant eels blocked her way. Behind them stood Hagema.

Most sea creatures who lived in the waters around Vancouver Island knew about Hagema. She was feared and hated, for she did many terrible things. Klee Wyck trembled as she saw her. Hagema was thin—very thin—with a slimy fishlike body. She wore a cloak made from the arms of a dead octopus, and her head was covered with decaying seaweed. Her eyes were black and beady, her gums toothless. In one of her lobster-claw hands she held the gold medal.

Klee Wyck gulped. "Please, Hagema, may I have my medal? And would you let Kia go? He's swum into your cave. He'll be terrified."

The witch cackled. "Your medal. No, you may not have it. Not that I want something that represents good sportsmanship and fair play. Ugh, the very thought of it! But *you* want the medal, and you want your brother back, too. You shall have them if you bring me what I want."

Hagema laughed as Kia, squealing with fright, tried to swim out of the cave. He was held back by a giant dogfish and the two eels, who were holding a large net. Turning her head, Hagema screeched, "Take him to the tank."

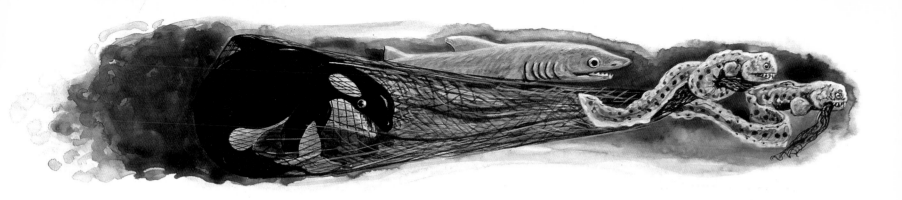

Klee Wyck was horrified. "Please, please let him go," she begged. "He'll drown if he gets no air. Let him go and you can keep my medal."

"Oh, he'll get air all right, unless I seal the tank. He'll even have a companion. Delphi, a dolphin who tried to trick me, is in the tank. But you can free your brother and have your medal. All you have to do is bring me three things."

"Three things. What three things?" asked the frightened young Orca.

The witch grinned, showing her blackened gums. "Magic things. Bring them to me, and I will be the most powerful creature within these waters. I want the silver telescope from Raven the Sly and the gold clamshell from Diablo the Demon Octopus. From Skara the Giant Troll of the North you will bring me the Book of Ocean Spells. The shell will enable me to hear the smallest whisper from here to the back of beyond. The telescope will allow me to see beyond the horizon, and with the book of spells I shall be able to rule the deep." She gave a horrible laugh and looked behind her. "Your brother is in my tank, and there he'll stay until the moon is full, five days from now. If by that time you don't bring what I have requested, I shall seal the tank, and he will die."

Klee Wyck was afraid. How would she find these things? But she made her voice defiant. "I will do what you ask, but don't you dare hurt my brother or Delphi. And keep my medal safe." But she talked to herself, for the witch had disappeared.

When Klee Wyck surfaced, her mother was waiting. "Where have you been?" Charlotte asked. "And where is Kia? I've been worried. You know you can't stay under water for too long at any one time. What were you doing? And—oh my goodness—where is your medal?"

Poor Klee Wyck. Almost in tears, she told her mother what had happened. Her mother gasped with horror. "Oh my goodness, what shall we do? Hagema is a terrible witch. Kia will be so frightened. We must go and try to rescue him. Perhaps if the whole pod went to see her . . ."

Klee Wyck shook her head. "No, Mother. If you do that, Hagema will surely put the lid on the tank. I must begin my quest now, but I really don't know where to begin. If only there were someone who could help."

Her mother brightened. "But there is. The Good Witch of the Sea. She's always very helpful. She lives at Long Beach, close to the north end of the long stretch of sand on the other side of the island. Hurry now."

Klee Wyck said a hasty goodbye and began to swim away. She felt very lonely without her family around, but the thought of Kia held captive kept her going.

Chapter Two

By the time Klee Wyck arrived at Long Beach, a three-quarter moon silvered the water and brightened the golden sands. She swam towards the point and dived down through the clear, green water. She easily found the underwater cave where the Good Witch lived. Two large, white rocks covered with colourful seashells stood on either side of the entrance to the cave. Several starfish were swimming around. "Hello, Klee Wyck," said one. "I suppose you want to see the Good Witch."

Klee Wyck nodded. A minute later the Good Witch of the Sea appeared. She was a giant mermaid, with a friendly, smiling face. Her head was covered with strands of fresh seaweed. Her eyes sparkled green, and her teeth shone like oyster pearls. As she swam towards Klee Wyck, her necklace of clamshells clicked.

"Klee Wyck. What can I do for you? You look very serious. Is something wrong? You're usually smiling. That's why your mother named you 'The Laughing One'." The Good Witch smiled. "I know. You've come to show me the Commonwealth Games Medal. You must be so proud to be mascot for the Games."

Klee Wyck hung her head. "I was proud, but now I've lost the medal. Hagema has it. Even worse, she's taken my brother Kia prisoner, and Delphi the dolphin, too."

The Good Witch was upset. "That's bad, very bad. But why has she done this?"

Quickly Klee Wyck explained. When she had finished, the eyes of the Good Witch flashed with anger. "Hagema is truly evil, but don't worry, I'll help you with your quest. You see, the magic things she has asked for once belonged to me. One day during a terrible storm, all three vanished from my cave. They were found by the Raven, the Octopus, and the Giant Troll. Those three are all scavengers. Of course they refused to give back my things. 'Finders keepers,' they said."

Klee Wyck sighed. "But how am I to get them back?"

The witch smiled, "Don't worry, Klee Wyck. Be positive and you'll succeed. Now, the first thing to do is get hold of Otty the Sea Otter. You'll need his help. Then find Great Eagle. You'll need him, too."

Swimming to the surface, Klee Wyck soon found the little sharp-toothed otter. Not long after, Great Eagle appeared in the sky. After telling her two friends the story, Klee Wyck dived down to the Good Witch. Otty went with her, while Great Eagle perched himself on top of a Douglas fir tree and waited.

The Good Witch had been casting some spells. With her long white fingers she attached two small shells to each of Klee Wyck's flippers. "When you need to be small," she instructed, "all you have to do is slap your left flipper three times against the water. You'll quickly shrink to Otty's size. To be your own size again, slap the other flipper the same way." She took two more clamshells from her necklace. Attaching one to each side of Klee Wyck's fluke she touched them with her trident. "These will give you great speed when you swim."

"Now for Otty. Open your mouth." The little sea otter opened his mouth, showing his sharp teeth. She touched the trident to his tongue. "This will make your tongue pointed, and as sharp as a razor. You will be able to help Klee Wyck if she runs into trouble."

Otty, who thought this was great fun, kept sticking his tongue out. "All right, Otty," said the Good Witch, "listen closely while I tell you about Raven the Sly. He lives at the top of the tallest fir tree on Nootka Island. He is very big and very tricky. He keeps the telescope in his nest, and when he is not there, his father, 'I Told You So,' keeps guard."

"That's a funny name," said Klee Wyck.

The Good Witch laughed. "That's because everytime anything goes wrong the old raven screams 'I told you so, I told you so'."

Otty chuckled, "Just like my mother."

"I expect so," said the Good Witch, knowing how mischievous Otty was. She turned and looked at Klee Wyck. "But you must watch out for him—he's as sly as his son. However, with the help of Great Eagle and Otty, I think you can outsmart Raven the Sly and his father. Here's what I think you should do."

Klee Wyck and Otty listened carefully. When she had finished, Otty clapped his paws together. "What a splendid plan," he shouted.

The Good Witch frowned. "Yes, it sounds easy, but don't forget Raven the Sly is a magic raven. Once he finds the telescope has gone, you will be in danger from one of his spells."

Thanking the Good Witch, Klee Wyck and Otty surfaced. With Great Eagle flying above them, they began their journey.

Chapter Three

Klee Wyck was a good, strong swimmer, even with Otty riding on her back. With the help of the magic fluke and a calm sea, they soon reached Nootka Sound. Only a little breeze stirred the giant fir trees. It was early morning and the beach was empty. It was littered with broken shells, kelp, bleached logs, and tree stumps. Otty scrambled ashore, and Great Eagle flew down to join him. They hid themselves behind a very large tree stump.

Klee Wyck swam out a little and then began to call.

"Raven," she squealed, "Raven the Sly." Nothing happened, so she called again. A minute later a huge black raven appeared on one of the lower branches of a tree.

"Good day, Raven," said Klee Wyck. "I am Klee Wyck, the Orca."

Raven pecked at his feathers, then flew down one more branch. "I can see you are an Orca," he chortled. "But what do you want with me? Why are you disturbing my rest with your horrible squealing?"

Klee Wyck, who was very polite, ignored the raven's rudeness. "I hear you have a magic telescope."

"Who told you that?" screamed Raven.

"Great Eagle." said Klee Wyck. "But he says your telescope is not the only magic one. He has one, too."

Raven the Sly flew off his perch onto the beach. "Nonsense," he bragged, "he is not telling the truth. I am the only one who has a magic silver telescope."

Klee Wyck turned over on her back and began to flipper lob, pretending to ignore Raven. This made Raven the Sly angry. He began to hop up and down on his skinny legs. "Where does he keep his telescope, Orca?"

Klee Wyck turned over again. "In his nest. But he says you don't have yours any more. You just pretend to have it."

Raven the Sly was now very angry. He ruffled his feathers and skipped up and down the beach. "Oh, he does, does he! Well, you just go back and tell him that's not so."

Klee Wyck dove down under the water, and the big black bird hopped even closer to the water's edge. When Klee Wyck surfaced she said, "I can't tell Great Eagle you have the telescope. I haven't seen it. I think he is right. You don't have it."

This was too much for Raven the Sly. Fluttering his dusty black feathers, he flew up into the tree. "Give me the telescope," he said to his father.

"What for?"

"Because there is an irritating Orca down there who says I do not have it. She says Great Eagle has one and I don't. So I'm going to show her mine."

"It's a trick," warned I Told You So.

"You're a silly old thing. I can deal with tricksters," boasted Raven the Sly.

This enraged I Told You So, who flew out of the nest cackling, "Mind your manners. Take your old telescope. But remember, I told you so."

Ignoring his father, Raven the Sly dove into the nest and emerged a minute later with the silver telescope in his beak. He flew to the edge of the beach and dropped it on the sand. "There," he said, "now go back and tell that stupid Eagle . . ." But he got no further. Great Eagle swooped out of the sky and caught Raven the Sly in his giant talons. At the same time Otty skipped out from behind the stump. He picked up the magic telescope in his teeth, slipped into the water, and swam out to where Klee Wyck was waiting.

Furious at being tricked, Raven the Sly let out a sharp cry. Within seconds the sky was filled with huge black ravens. Great Eagle released the sly bird, who immediately flew up and pecked forcefully at Great Eagle's yellow eyes. For a moment Great Eagle was blinded. The sky was black with ravens. Large ones, small ones, old ones, and young ones, they flew at Great Eagle. They clawed at his wings and tried to force him down onto the beach.

Meanwhile, Raven the Sly hopped onto a log and screamed angrily at Klee Wyck. "Bring back the telescope or we shall kill Great Eagle."

Klee Wyck, who loved her friend, was about to ask Otty to swim back with it when Great Eagle summoned his enormous strength, beat back the ravens, and began to fly. With his great wings spread, he rose high into the blue sky and flew off over the ocean. He dipped his wings as he passed over his two friends, and Klee Wyck squealed a big "thank you."

Before she left, Klee Wyck looked back at the beach. There was Raven the Sly, hopping up and down angrily while his father kept scolding, "I told you so, I told you so."

Klee Wyck laughed. She was happy. The first part of her quest was over. Perhaps the rest would be as easy. But she wasn't so happy once they returned to the Good Witch of the Sea, who told them about Diablo, the Demon Octopus.

"Diablo is the biggest, meanest octopus in the whole of the west coast waters. He is a demon octopus, who lives in a sunken Spanish vessel near Barkley Sound. He is even more wicked than Hagema," said the Good Witch. Klee Wyck and Otty shivered. The Good Witch smiled. "It's not a bad thing to be afraid," she said. "It makes you more careful, and this time you will need to be very careful."

"Where is the ship and where does Diablo keep the shell?" asked Klee Wyck.

"The ship is a man-of-war and lies near the rocks where the giant sea lions live. They will help you find the vessel. They hate Diablo. But you may have to feed them some fish before they tell you where it is. They are quite greedy."

"And fat," said Otty. "I know one of them. She's called Sabrina. She's huge."

The Good Witch continued her advice. "The gold clamshell is in the gun barrel of a cannon. It's guarded by a whole army of hagfish and eels—small but dangerous creatures. They will make the shell hard enough to reach, but even worse, Diablo never sleeps. He only takes small naps."

Klee Wyck gulped. "How can I get into the gun barrel of a cannon?"

"Use the magic in your flippers and make yourself small like me," suggested Otty.

"Of course," agreed Klee Wyck. "Then we'll both get in the barrel. Let's start our journey right away."

The Good Witch sighed. "I wish it were easier. Take care. I shall watch you through the magic telescope. If you run into danger, I shall try to help. Now, off with you, for in another three days the moon will be full."

Chapter Four

*I*t was dusk by the time the two friends surfaced. Klee Wyck swam swiftly towards Barkley Sound and soon reached the place where the sea lions lived. The adults were spread out over the rocks, sleeping and snoring. The younger ones chased each other in and out amongst small islands. Their sleek bodies glistened and their big round eyes sparkled with fun.

On one of the bigger rocks, three of the largest sea lions, stellar seals, flapped their flippers and barked at each other. They made a terrible din. "Sabrina and her two brothers," said Otty gloomily. "They're quarreling again. We'll have to wait till they quiet down."

Almost as if they'd heard him, the three seals suddenly flopped down, spread themselves out, and prepared for sleep. Nervously Klee Wyck swam closer. Otty swam around the rock, and Klee Wyck began to spy hop, her big black and white head rising and bobbing in the water.

Otty had been right, thought Klee Wyck. Sabrina was a very large, fat sea lion. She was half asleep. Her whiskers twitched. Klee Wyck let out a squeal. Sabrina's eyes opened. "Sir," squealed Klee Wyck a second time.

"Are you addressing me, young Orca?" barked Sabrina. "If so, it's madam, not sir."

"Sorry, madam," apologized Klee Wyck. "I wonder if you can help me?"

"Help you. Not until I've had my supper. I'm much too hungry to help anyone."

"I could get you a salmon," offered Klee Wyck, hoping there were some salmon around.

"Sockeye," said Sabrina. "Three."

Klee Wyck was lucky. Within a few minutes she returned carrying three fat sockeye salmon in her mouth.

"Bring them here, Orca," ordered Sabrina.

Klee Wyck swam closer and tossed the salmon onto the rock. Greedily Sabrina began to eat, ignoring the other two sea lions who were now awake and giving her hungry looks.

In between swallowing and twitching her whiskers, Sabrina found time to ask Klee Wyck what she wanted. "To find the wreck where Diablo the Demon Octopus lives," answered Klee Wyck.

"That's easily done," barked Sabrina. "Though why anyone would want to find that horrible demon I don't know. We know exactly where he lives, and we keep away." She turned to the largest of her two brothers, "Benjie, go and get Oscar." Benjie slid his huge body into the water and swam away, returning a minute later with a young, mischievous looking seal. "My son," announced Sabrina.

"Hello, Oscar," called Otty, appearing from behind the rock.

"Hi, Otty. Is this your friend?"

Otty nodded. "That's Klee Wyck. We need to find the ship where Diablo lives."

Sabrina, who was now sitting up licking her flippers with her tongue, interrupted. "You know where the ship is, Oscar. That horrible demon almost caught you last year. All I want you to do is show them where it is. Don't you go with them. Understand?"

"Yes, Mamma." The young seal looked at Otty. "Guess you want to go right now?"

"Please," chimed Klee Wyck and Otty in unison.

After thanking Sabrina, Klee Wyck began to follow Otty and Oscar. The little otter and the young seal were old friends and chattered away together. But as soon as the moon appeared from behind a bank of clouds, Klee Wyck looked up and thought about her little brother Kia and Delphi the dolphin. How awful to be a prisoner. Not to be free to enjoy the wonders of the sea. Not to be with family and friends.

Klee Wyck shuddered, thinking about Hagema. Then she thought about her gold medal and what it meant to be the Commonwealth Games mascot. She loved to compete with the other young Orcas in speed swimming, and she leapt the highest in breaching competitions. She always did her best to win, but if she lost she still smiled. Klee Wyck would free her brother and Delphi and wear the medal to the opening of the Games. She began to swim with new determination.

However, at that very moment Diablo was listening to the sounds coming from the golden clamshell. Diablo was not a pretty sight. He was crawling along the ocean bottom supported by three of his eight arms. These long, thick, slithery arms were covered with suckers. Each sucker was filled with a poison that paralysed shellfish before they were captured. Diablo loved shellfish but today he'd just eaten a mass of small fish. His big, black, ugly body with its sac full of inky poison lurched along towards home.

The wrecked man-of-war lay on its side. Hundreds of little fish, eels, and small octopus, dogfish, and jellyfish swam in and out of its rotting hatches. The cannon, rusted and covered with a green, slimy substance, lay on a lower deck. It was guarded by two giant eels. Inside, it swarmed with creatures called hagfish.

As Diablo approached, all the fish except the two giant eels disappeared. Everyone feared him. "Something is coming," announced Diablo. He had a whistling, whispery voice, like the wind when it whistles down the chimney. "Something big. An Orca, I think. Take the clamshell and put it back in its hiding place." He gave a horrible chuckle. "No Orca can get into the barrel of that cannon."

The two giant eels laughed with him. Two smaller eels appeared from the depths of the ship, wrapped themselves around the shell, and disappeared into the gun barrel.

"Good," said Diablo. "Now let's wait for our visitor."

Meanwhile, Klee Wyck and Otty, led by Oscar, had dived down and found the wreck. Oscar

wanted to stay, but Klee Wyck, remembering Sabrina's ˙ ˙ ˙ ers, told him he must go home. All three returned to the surface, and reluctantly the little stellar seal swam back home.

A small school of fish passed by. Klee Wyck ignored her hunger and politely asked them if they had seen Diablo. The fish swam past without even answering. "I'll go and see if I can find the cannon," said Otty.

Otty dove under and soon was peering inside the wreck. He retreated when two giant eels swam towards him. Otty shook them off and returned to Klee Wyck. "The gun barrel is full of hagfish and eels," he told her. "But I thought I saw a glimpse of something gold. I didn't see Diablo, but I saw two giant eels."

"I'm sure the demon is around, Otty, but he won't be expecting a tiny Orca." Klee Wyck slapped her left flipper against the water three times. In a second she was no bigger than Otty.

The two friends glided down into the wreck. Diablo heard them and slithered in their direction. A minute later Klee Wyck and Otty were enveloped in an inky black liquid. "Close your mouth," warned Otty. "It's poisonous. Try to surface." Spluttering and spitting, the two friends rose to the surface once again.

"That got rid of them," chuckled Diablo. "What that black and white creature was, I don't know. They both looked quite tasty." But before he could eat more he needed to digest the scrumptious meal of fish he had eaten on his way home. He would take a quick nap. Diablo attached himself to the rotting keel and went to sleep.

Cautiously Klee Wyck and Otty dove down once again to the wreck. This time they went straight to the cannon. "Quiet," whispered Otty as he saw the two giant eels stretched out and making small snoring noises.

"I'll go into the barrel first," said Klee Wyck, "while you stand guard." Inside, it was dark and horrid. All around her Klee Wyck could feel creatures stirring. In a second her body was covered with small eels, but she kept on swimming towards the glint of gold she could see below her.

The gold clamshell was covered with jelly-like hagfish. They were piled one upon the other on the shell. As Klee Wyck approached, they swam to meet her. Three of them swam right into her blowhole. Now Klee Wyck couldn't breathe. Below her she could see the prized gold shell, but she was choking and sinking.

Otty, seeing his friend in trouble, swam into the gun barrel and began prodding at the hagfish with his magic tongue. Jab, jab, jab he went, as the eels blocked his progress. And pop, pop, pop went the hagfish. Soon he was above Klee Wyck, who was barely breathing. In a second he had popped all the hagfish in her blowhole until they were nothing but watery blobs. Quickly he dove past Klee Wyck and picked up the clamshell with his paws.

Klee Wyck and Otty swam out of the gun barrel. Diablo and the eels were waiting for them. Once more Diablo let loose the inky poison, but this time Otty swam furiously through the blue-black cloud, while Klee Wyck slapped her right flipper against the water. In a minute she reached her full size and knocked Diablo and the two eels back against the deck of the ship.

By the time Diablo had recovered, Otty and Klee Wyck had surfaced. With the aid of the magic fluke they swam rapidly back towards the Good Witch.

Chapter Five

*T*he Good Witch was delighted to see Klee Wyck and Otty again. After thanking them for the return of the shell, she immediately told her two friends about Skara the Giant Troll. "I've tried looking for him through the telescope," she said, "but I can't find him. He no longer lives in the ocean. Now he lives north of Vancouver Island on an abandoned island. Part of the Queen Charlottes. He makes his home in a cave, deep in the heart of a dense wood. He came from far away, a long, long time ago. He is very old."

Puzzled, Klee Wyck asked how she could get to the Giant Troll on land. "I'm a sea mammal," she protested.

"With magic, all things are possible," smiled the witch. Taking her silver trident, she touched Klee Wyck's fluke. "There, that will do it." She sighed. "But that's all the magic I can give you this time. However, you two have already proven to be a good team. I'm sure you'll come back with the Book of Ocean Spells."

Otty was curious. "How big is the Giant Troll?"

"Tall and big," said the Good Witch. "Almost as tall as a giant fir tree."

Otty whistled through his teeth. "Wow, that's pretty tall. Is he very fierce?"

"Don't know," answered the witch. "I've never really had much to do with him. He has a reputation for being fierce. He keeps a giant shark for a pet. He brought it back from the South Pacific. It's a nasty looking creature that lives in an underwater cave close to the shore. Skara's own cave, deep in the woods, is guarded by two white wolves."

"Do you know where he keeps the book?" asked Klee Wyck.

The Good Witch shook her head. "I'm not sure. It could be anywhere. You'll have to search."

Otty looked glum. "This is going to be hard."

Klee Wyck nodded. "But we'd better hurry and go. Tomorrow night the moon will be full."

The two friends said goodbye to the Good Witch and began their journey to the Queen Charlotte Islands. The moon turned the ocean to silver. On the shore the fir trees sighed and fluttered their branches. A gentle wind blew. As Klee Wyck and Otty drew near their destination, the islands appeared ghostly and mysterious.

Swimming in between the islands and the reefs, Klee Wyck could see many small islands. They all looked deserted. On some of them she could see tall, dark shapes against the sky. "They're totem poles," said Otty. "Carved with heads of wilderness creatures like you and me."

Klee Wyck wondered on which island the troll lived. She spotted two cormorants sitting on a floating log. "Do you know where the Giant Troll of the North lives?"

The cormorants were friendly. "Over there, I think," said the bigger one, pointing to a heavily wooded small island. "Anyway, I wouldn't go too near if I were you. There's a big white shark who patrols up and down the shore." His feathers fluttered as he shivered. "Nasty looking creature. Huge teeth. Ugh."

Klee Wyck's heart sank. How would they get past the shark? As if reading her thoughts Otty said, "Tell you what, I'll go and disturb the creature, and while he's distracted by me, you climb onto the shore and try and find the troll."

Klee Wyck waited while Otty swam away. A minute later she saw a big white shape flash through the water and move towards the other side of the island. Quickly she swam to shore. Using her fluke she pulled herself onto the beach just as Otty, puffing and panting, scrambled ashore. "Wow!" said Otty. "That shark is awesome. Bet he's still looking for me."

Klee Wyck decided to try to walk. Otty looked on with amazement as she drew herself up. She was almost as tall as a small Douglas fir.

They walked up the beach to the wood. A fine mist engulfed the island. The thickly clustered trees dripped moisture. It was dark and scary. A terrible noise erupted, which made Klee Wyck and Otty freeze. It sounded like a thunderclap. It was followed by another clap and then another. Otty shivered and crept closer to Klee Wyck. The leaves on the trees trembled. So did Klee Wyck.

As Klee Wyck and Otty moved through the wood, the sound got louder and louder. They could see the entrance to a very large cave and they could see the two white wolves. The wolves began to howl. They spotted Klee Wyck and Otty and leapt towards them, teeth bared. Otty ran quickly into the cave, but Klee Wyck was trapped.

A voice thundered and the earth shook. "Tanoo, Agedar, stop that noise. Why did you wake me up when I was enjoying a good snore? What's the matter? Do we have a visitor?" The two wolves stopped snarling and slunk to the side of the largest creature Klee Wyck had ever seen.

Skara the Giant Troll was at least a head taller than Klee Wyck. He had a lumpy, bumpy face, a squashed nose, and one large grey eye in the middle of his forehead. He had big pointed ears, a long grey beard, and a thick clump of hair that stood up on his head like a small bush. He smiled. Klee Wyck could see three yellowed teeth. He was wearing a long shirt made from eelskin, with pockets on either side. In one of the pockets Klee Wyck could see a book.

The giant held up a lantern and peered at Klee Wyck. His voice sounded like the rumbling of a terrible storm. "And who are you that dares to come to the island of Skara the Troll?"

"Klee Wyck," whispered the terrified Orca.

"Klee Wyck is it then? 'The Laughing One.' Once there was a lady named Emily Carr, who the Indians called 'Klee Wyck.' She often came to these islands to paint pictures of the totem poles." Skara smiled. "And I see you're an Orca. A walking Orca. Are you a witch, a magician, or a spirit?"

"None of those," said Klee Wyck nervously. "The Good Witch of the Sea made magic so that I could come to see you. I need your help."

Skara frowned and looked a bit puzzled. "So you've come to visit me?" He sighed. "At one time these islands had a lot of people on them. No more though. These days I don't get many visitors and I do like a bit of company. It's really not much fun being a giant troll. Most creatures are afraid of me. Are you?"

Klee Wyck hesitated, "Well, just a little. I think my friend Otty's very afraid. He's hiding in your cave."

"In my cave! Well, let's hope he and Orsa have made friends."

"Orsa?"

The giant smiled. "My pet bear. She's really quite nice. She just looks fierce. Come along. Let's go inside and talk about how I can help you."

Klee Wyck followed Skara into the cave. Everywhere it was dark, but when the giant held up his lamp Klee Wyck could see huge grey granite walls covered with a green moss. Skara lit another lamp and Klee Wyck looked around for Otty. Her little friend was nowhere to be seen.

Orsa, a big black bear, glared at Klee Wyck, but the giant patted the bear's head. "Now now, Orsa, this is Klee Wyck. She's come to see me because she needs my help. It's nice to be needed, you know." His eye looked up and down and around the cave. "What have you done with her friend Otty?"

"He's under your bed," growled Orsa.

At the mention of his name, Otty poked his head out from under a bed made from enormous logs and covered with fir branches. "Is it safe to come out?"

Skara bent down and picked Otty up, holding him gently in two giant paws.

"Don't worry little fellow," he said. "You'll come to no harm here. Now let's sit down, and we can all listen while Klee Wyck tells me why you are both here."

He pointed to a giant tree stump. Klee Wyck sat down and began to tell her story. She told the troll all about Hagema, Kia, Delphi, and the medal, but when she came to the part about the Book of Ocean Spells Skara again looked angry. "That's my book," he roared, shaking the earth. "I found it,

and you know what they say, 'Finders Keepers, Losers Weepers'." He scratched his head and frowned. "But that witch. She's a nasty piece of work!" He coughed apologetically. "Mind you, I've done a few nasty things in my time, but nothing like that horrible creature."

Skara stood up and walked about the cave, each step sounding like a roll of thunder. "But let's think how I can help you rescue your brother and Delphi and get back your medal. You can have the book. It's really awfully boring—just a lot of spells I don't need, especially now that I spend most of my time on land." He took it from his pocket and was about to give it to Otty when he stopped. "Just a minute," he said. "I've remembered something. There's a spell in this book—something about getting rid of a wicked sea witch."

He began to leaf through the book. "Now, where was it?" His face brightened. "Ah, there it is under 'W.' Now, let's see what it says. Hmm . . . splendid. Oh, no . . . difficult. Hmm . . . easy. Perhaps." He looked up and grinned. "I think we can do it. We'll rescue Kia, Delphi, and the medal. Then the Good Witch can have her Book of Ocean Spells."

He fixed Otty and Klee Wyck with a stare from his big grey eye. "But you must promise to do something for me if the plan works." Klee Wyck swallowed. She did hope he wasn't going to ask something difficult. But then Skara grinned. "It's all right." He patted her head, "I just want you to come back and visit and tell me all about the Commonwealth Games."

Klee Wyck sighed with relief. "Of course I'll come. But it's almost full moon. If we don't hurry, Hagema will put the lid on the tank. Please, Mr. Skara."

"Don't worry," said the troll. "Here's what we need for the spell to work. First, the silver trident from the Good Witch, then a pod of Orcas, and last, a full moon. Simple. Come on, let's get going. I'll tell you on the way how it will work. I think I'll bring Sheba along for company." Klee Wyck and Otty were both about to ask who Sheba was when Skara said, "My friend, the great white shark. You must have seen her on the way here. Between you and me, she's quite harmless."

"Like you," said Otty boldly, as they left the cave. The big troll laughed, and all the trees shook. The white wolves padded along behind them. When they got to the water's edge, Sheba greeted her master with a toothy grin that made Otty scuttle closely to Klee Wyck.

"Don't be afraid," said Skara. "Now, what shall I be? It's ages since I was in the water. I think I'll become an Orca." He turned himself around three times, then bowed to the east and west and said some funny words. Seconds later, there in the water was a big black and white Orca.

Klee Wyck could hardly believe her eyes. "Why, you look just like me."

"But a bit bigger," laughed the troll. "Come along then, we've got work to do."

Chapter Six

*J*ust before the full moon rose, Skara, Sheba, Klee Wyck, and Otty reached the cave of the Good Witch. They handed her the Book of Ocean Spells. After listening to their story she offered Skara the silver trident.

"Would you like to come along?" Skara asked.

"Oh, yes," laughed the Good Witch. "It will be a pleasure to see the end of Hagema."

"Next," said Skara, "we must find Klee Wyck's pod."

"That's easy," advised Klee Wyck. "They'll be at Johnstone Strait, close to Hagema's cave."

"Excellent," said Skara, "by the time we get there the moon will be full. Now here's what we must do."

The full moon had risen in the night sky when Skara, disguised as an Orca, dove down to Hagema's lair. The witch, surrounded by her pet eels, was waiting. She was shortsighted and peered into the gloomy waters. "Ah ha. Klee Wyck. Where are my things? Your brother Kia and that Delphi are becoming a nuisance. I shall be glad to put the lid on the tank and rid myself of them. So, where's the shell and the telescope and the book? Time's up. The moon is full. I want them NOW, understand?"

What a hateful creature, thought Skara. Pretending to be Klee Wyck, he imitated her voice. "Please, Hagema, I couldn't bring them with me. My mother, Charlotte, has them. If you come to the surface with me she'll give them to you."

Hagema let out a horrible shriek. "If this is a trick, your brother will die. I'll come to the surface, but I won't release Kia or Delphi or give you the medal until I have what I sent you to get. My eels will stand guard until I return. Understand?"

Skara didn't answer, but began to swim to the surface. The wicked, greedy witch followed. The minute she surfaced, the whole pod of whales surrounded her, making a magic circle. Then they began to sing the Song of The Sea. Hagema tried to break the spell by diving back under the ocean, but she stopped as she saw Sheba just below her. Once more her head rose above the surface.

Now the Good Witch swam into the circle. Taking her silver trident, she touched the top of Hagema's head once, twice, thrice, and then a fourth time. There was a terrible flash and a great shriek. The wind rose, and the sea grew choppy. Overhead, a cloud covered the moon. A minute later the cloud passed, the wind dropped, and the ocean calmed. Hagema had vanished.

The pod cheered, while Klee Wyck, together with Skara and Otty, dove down to release Kia and Delphi. Without Hagema, the eels slithered quickly away. Only her two prisoners and Klee Wyck's gold medal hanging on a piece of kelp remained in Hagema's lair.

What a party there was that night, as Kia joined his mother, and Delphi swam home to her family. Otty, Skara, Sheba, and the Good Witch joined the pod in a feast of salmon and herring. Great Eagle flew overhead and dipped his wings in greeting.

Klee Wyck, wearing her gold medal again, joined the other young Orcas in a breaching competition. She was so full of happiness she leapt further out of the water than she had ever done before. "A new record," said Charlotte, to which the Good Witch added, "A true Commonwealth Games champion."

The sun was rising when the Good Witch and Otty took their leave. A little later, Skara and Sheba began their journey to the Queen Charlottes. Klee Wyck waved goodbye to them. Skara had become a good friend, and she was sorry to see him go. Before he left he touched Klee Wyck's gold medal. "You are a brave and good Orca. You deserve this medal, and you are a fine mascot for the Commonwealth Games. Now don't forget to come and see me and tell me all about the different sporting events, the athletes, and the festivities."

"I won't forget," promised Klee Wyck.

On the opening day of the Friendly Games no one could have been happier than Klee Wyck wearing her gold medal. She watched as the athletes from the Commonwealth countries walked proudly around the stadium. Seeing them, she thought about her family, Skara, Otty, Great Eagle, and the Good Witch. And remembering her quest, Klee Wyck understood the true spirit of friendship.

Victoria 94™
XV Commonwealth Games
XV Jeux du Commonwealth

Victoria, British Columbia, will host the XV Commonwealth Games, Canada's largest sporting event of the decade, from August 18 to 28, 1994. Klee Wyck, Official Mascot of the Games, will be there to welcome 3,200 athletes from 66 Commonwealth nations.

Klee Wyck's Magic Quest